WORDS FROM AN ANGEL
PART 1
2 PART SERIES

© Copyright PETER JAMES LJUNG
2019

A swedish nurse discovers she has more than just the kind face and dedication that hospitals look for.
She is taken on a journey of love and shown a world of wonder that she did not know existed.
Join Lindsy as she is introduced to a science fiction that becomes science fact.
A spiritual science fiction thriller with a great love story.

WORDS FROM AN ANGEL PART 1

WORDS FROM AN ANGEL
PART 1
A TWO-PART SERIES
by
Peter James Ljung

Chapter 1
Lindsy Strömberg

Nearly every woman is looking for true love sometimes in their life, and I am no different.

My name is Lindsy Strömberg. Let me tell you my unbelievable and remarkable story.

"All good things come to those who wait." So, someone once said.

At thirty years old, I'm in a pretty good position financially and materially. I have a nearly brand new BMW sports convertible, my own apartment, and this is all paid for by my everyday job.

My job is a nurse in the accident and emergency rooms at the university hospital in Borås Sweden.

I believe that without using vanity, I am a fairly average looking blond Swedish girl.

Many would be boyfriends from the past would tell me, " I was so sexy and lovable," but then most of them would tell me that just to extract my underwear, I managed to keep that cage closed until I turned twenty-two years old.

Yes! After I lost my virginity, I needed to prove to myself that there must be better sex than what I experienced. I could tell you all the sordid and raunchy things that happened the first time, but, I won't bore you with the groans and moans of a five-minute wonder and a guy who had an ego the size of a river!

I had no idea that a few years later in life I would find my knight in shining armor.

Obviously! you're reading this now, so, you have

discovered my secret diary. What I'm about to
tell you will turn your world upside down! It will also
reveal some wonderful emotions and
 feelings I had searching for my soul mate. Do soul
mates really exist? For a long time, I doubted
 that. I thought that mine had been kidnapped by
aliens or took a wrong turning one day and
 missed me by miles!
After my first full sexual intercourse encounter, I began
to question things. Was this what all the
fuss was about? I felt badly let down.
My dreams were quite simple really!
In my first thirty years of life, I wanted to have a drivers
license, a better home, a beautiful
loving man to greet me after work, a wonderful baby
boy or girl. To have a great job, but
something more than just a job. I wanted so much to
make a difference in the world.
I got the license, bought a fantastic apartment in town.
Passing all my nursing exams was my
dream come true. With plenty of cash pouring into my
bank account, I could afford the BMW
sports car.
My Mom was a tower of strength in my life, she would
always put my Father and me first in
everything, as long as we were happy, she was
happy.
Dad was quite reserved most of the time, he would
come home from work, do his daily chores,
then relax for the rest of the day saying next to
nothing.
I guess the day he came home and asked to speak to

both Mom and me at the dinner table was
Unexpected.
That day gave me the first heart-ache pain that I had
never felt until then.
I remember his soft-spoken words as we sat around the
table wondering what was so important
 to warrant a family discussion.
" Elizebeth! Lindsy!, this isn't going to be easy, but for
the last few months I've been seeing a
 heart and lung specialist in Göteborg, I haven't
mentioned anything until now. Today I saw the
heart specialist, he told me that nothing can be done!
He told me to go and put my affairs in
order and be with my family for what little time I have
left in this world!"
Silence fell in the house. Mom looked at Dad, then me.
If tears had sounded when they moved,
they would have sounded like rolling thunder as clouds
crashed into each other.
For Mom, It was like someone announcing the end of
the world, I came a close second with
those feelings.
Very slowly and shaking with the news, we both
moved towards Dad, and then with our six
arms threw them around each other and holding on to
dear life.
Tear droplets fell by our feet, some dripped onto our
shoes, then trickled on to the tiled floor
forming small water pools. I noticed through my misty
damp eyes Dad holding Moms hand so
tight, the color was draining from her skin. She had
turned ashen white, her face looked like I

had never seen it before. Mom looked so powerless as
we continued to hug each other hard, no
one said anything for what seemed like an eternity.
After several minutes just standing and holding each
other, all of us lost for any words to say, we
 still held each other tightly as we moved to the couch.
Like the weight of a truck of cement, we all fell to the
fabric on the large seating area, then loud
sobbing from all three of us drowned the silence as we
still said nothing.
That very day, I can honestly say I was thinking so
many selfish thoughts, with every beat of my
heart, I believed it was mine that was going to give up
on me, It hurt so damn bad. What was I
going to do without my dear, dear father? I had
enough self-pity for the whole of Sweden that
day.

I had never attended a funeral before, so standing at
the graveside dressed in black along with
sweet Mom was like I was living that day in a fantasy
world where nothing made sense and felt
empty.
Dad was a well-respected man, a kind caring sensitive
man who would have done anything for
anyone. Mom moved to the closed coffin resting on the
chrome poles before it was to be lowered
into the two-meter trench.
Very slowly and gently, she placed two red roses, then
a pure brilliant white rose in between
Them, tears once again fell from her glistening eyes
and splattered over the roses and the coffin.

Mom leaned forward and placed her pink moist lips
and gave Dad the final farewell kiss he so
deserved.
Many wonderful sayings Dad used in his life, he one
hundred percent respected other people,
especially women!
He told many men through time how "women were
very special and deserved to be treated with
respect and dignity."
I remember one time Dad came out with a saying that
surprised me tremendously.
He said. " Every woman is special! Each one is like a
golden jig-saw puzzle. Every piece is
bright with golden sparkles, It takes a long long time to
find the right pieces and place them in
the correct position, but, when they fit, the puzzle
takes on a beautiful outcome and reveals a
wonderful picture of a special human being." Dad
certainly had a way with words at times, those
 words of wisdom were straight from his heart. God! I
was going to miss him so much.
Mom shortly after that heartbreaking period in our life,
decided to move back up to the Northern
Part of Sweden. We talked long and hard about that
subject, but, I was happy she was going to
do what was right for her, and I could always drive up
to visit.
For me, Borås was where my roots were grounded.
Dads departure left a gaping hole in me. Life does go
on though, and as best as we could, Mom
and I picked up the broken pieces in our lives.
The house we had lived in for many years was in a

sought after area in Borås, so we were
surprised when Mom got offered six million Swedish
Krona which had doubled from when Dad
and Mom bought it.
More surprising was when I got home from the hospital
after a long night shift, then discovered a
bankers draft on the dining table with the words "
Lindsy". She had made it out for two million
Krona with a note that read. " My beautiful daughter! I
will not take no for an answer, you will
take this money and buy yourself an apartment or
house for yourself, also treat yourself to a
vacation and a nice new car." If someone had a
feather, they could have knocked me over with
it! No kidding!
There was no arguing with Mom, so with a brand new
smile on my face, I accepted it with
Gratitude.
I think there are some wonderful people in this world,
all though you could be forgiven for
thinking otherwise with all the terrorism and violence in
the world.
Most of the good ones work within the caring and
hospital industries. The university hospital in
Borås has a dedicated staff of doctors and nurses who
will bend over backward to make sure the
patient is given the care they deserve.
Like any emergency room, you just never know when
everyone can be up to their eyes in the
 wall to wall patients.
At work, I have two close friends, both women, and
when we get together, we are like demons

who have been let out of hell for the night, no town is safe when Sasha, Suzan and I go
partying.

Chapter 2
The country singer

I'm not sure why the three of us ended up in a
nightclub in town where they had a country and
western group playing. I absolutely hate this type of
music. Always have!
I wanted to party, have fun, maybe meet a cool guy,
but I couldn't see how this night was going
to help with that.
I now know that sometimes in life, circumstances
present themselves in the strangest ways.
"Let's make the most of now!" Said, Sasha, with a
broad smile on her face. The smile was wide
as she had taken quite a lot of vodka before we left
the apartment. Our Dutch courage medicine,
so to speak.
Suzan glanced over at me standing just behind
Sasha, then smiled and raised her right-hand
index finger to the side of her head, pulled her thumb
back and pretended to shoot herself. You
could tell Sasha was quite intoxicated, there was no
way she was going to last the
entire night.
The three of us surveyed the nightclub. Many men
and women were beginning to fill the entire
dancehall. Ages varied, but most were in their late
thirties or more. Alcohol was flowing faster as
people waited for their beverages.
Guitars, drums, double bass and acoustic guitars
started to tune up getting ready for their
 Performance.
" One two! Testing one two three " Came the female
voice standing center stage. The hall
speakers crackled and hissed as the sound crew fine-
tuned the apparatus.

" Good evening, ladies and gentlemen, we will be starting in about ten minutes, refresh your drinks and get comfortable for a great nights entertainment."

Lindsy looked up and towards the stage where all the performers were, her ears had picked up something in the females voice. The voice was unusual, it was emanating a vibration, a tone so harmonious, it vibrated around Linsy,s body and penetrated her senses.

Lindsy shrugged the feeling off as silly and stupid, actually, she had no idea as to what just happened.

Only a few moments passed, most people were now seated and busy talking and waiting expectantly for the night to start and come to life. Beating drums echoed in the large nightclub as the drummer started on the snare drum, then with the brass symbols clanging into life. The sound technicians pressed buttons and sliders to give an electronic flute effect. It was almost like they had an entire orchestra in the background. The double bass joined in with its deep humming tones, followed closely by the acoustic and bass guitars.

The sounds all blended together like a perfect cake mix. Adding each ingredient together blending tones and harmonies in such a way, this country music seemed so different to what Lindsy was used to.

Then it happened!. The female singer center stage looked at the audience and smiled, opened her mouth to sing, what came from her vocal chords was absolutely incredible. Lindsy once again looked directly at her, she was mesmerized, almost hypnotized by the sounds softly and

gently being exhaled from her throat.
" You have always been there for me. I just didn't
realize how close you were. I have loved you
Forever, my heart you make it stir." The voice was so
beautiful, every single person listened
intently as she sang line after line of a wonderful
country song.
Lindsy was fixated on the face of the female singer.
From a short distance to the stage, she gazed
hard and listened as musical vibrations from her
voice, activated something deep inside her.
" What the hell is happening to me?" She asked
herself.
Still watching every move from the singer, she found
she couldn't take her gaze off her. Inside
her entire body, tingling and sparking sensations
could be felt with an unseen power.
Atoms and molecules collided with an unseen soul.
Stirring emotional feelings that Lindsy
never knew she had, came to life. In turn, these
feelings headed to her beautiful eyes.
Teardrops slowly trickled down her cheeks, gathering
together on her quaint chin, then fell
slowly to the table where all three girls were sitting.
Both her friends hadn't noticed Lindsy dripping
glistening tears. There was so much moisture in
her eye sockets, her vision started to get blurry. With
the colored spotlights on the country group
on stage, magnificent spectrums of light emitted from
the bright lights. In Lindsy`s eyes, there
were dancing shapes of every color, and colors that
she had never seen before.
Metalic silvery greys, fluorescent purples and mixed
together with vibrant wisps of mercury
molecules. The crazy thing was, that subliminal
messages were being guided to her very soul.

Lindsy just knew deep within her that she was exactly where she was supposed to be at that point in time. Wiping her tears slowly from her eyes, she smiled a little at the singer in front of her.

Almost instantaneously, the singer moved her bright blue eyes reflected by the spot lamps and smiled at Lindsy, still singing in fantastic musical tones. " You are the answer to some prayers, you are here to heal with the love in your heart!" The last lines from her first song ended, then loud applause erupted from the audience as most of them raised to their feet clapping long and hard. Lindsy also stood up and brought her hands together, and once again choked back her tears as they rolled down into her throat, taking her breath away a little as they did so.

In a split second, she decided she had been awakened into the country music scene. Something inside her was connected to a beautiful energy, and that energy was radiating from the female before her.

Song after song was sung over several minutes. Some people got up and danced, but Lindsy just sat there facing this wonderful singer.

It was only about forty minutes into the entertainment when Suzan suggested that she take Sasha

home as she was well drunk.

" Are you coming with us, Lindsy? Or stay for a while?"

" If its ok with you, I will stay Suzan!" Lindsy replied. Under normal circumstances, I would not have thought twice about leaving a country venue, but, then this night was far from being normal. Every inch of my body inside and out was vibrating.

Refreshing my vodka coke drink from the bar, I

returned to my table, now empty of my two friends.

Without hearing the changeover, disco music had started as the group were taking a refreshment for thirty minutes.

I was staring at the ice cubes slowly dissolving in the dark black drink. Bubbles forced their way to the surface and fizz popped.

" Do you mind if I sit with you? " Came the soft-spoken females voice standing directly in front of the table.

I must admit I was a little startled when I heard those words, but without even thinking, I replied.

" Oh yes! Please do," Wondering why this beautiful country singer wanted to sit with me?

" I am Cina! " She held out her hand for the gesture of greeting each other.

" Hello, Cina! I am Lindsy, nice to meet you.

Sitting down opposite Lindsy was this dazzling thirty-something, blond lady.

As both their hands gripped each other, Lindsy felt an overwhelming surge of energy running the entire length of her right arm.

" My first song opened your mind earlier Lindsy!?" She asked with a wonderful glowing smile on her face. Cina,s Face glowed in the semi-dark club.

" As I sang, I had been drawn to you watching me. I saw your eyes glistening, and then saw some tears run from your eyes. " Lindsy blushed a little when hearing those words from her, but, smiled slightly back at her letting Cina know she was right.

" I have to be honest with you, Cina! I have always disliked country music in the past, but, tonight something happened, and I can't explain it."

I watched Cina broaden her smile more as I answered her. She was still holding my hand. There was something magnetic bonding our fingers, and as much as I thought I should remove it, I couldn't.

" Just in case you are worried Lindsy, I am not gay, I have a wonderful man in my life, sometimes, however, I am drawn to certain people with a look that I find impossible to turn away from." Cina continued.

" Singing is a big part of my life. I was told by my Mom to sing from the heart, and that's what I try to do. I also know great things come to those I'm drawn to, and tonight, you are one of those people."

I began to relax and started to let go of the anxiety that was running through my mind. Still focusing on Cina's eyes, I knew what she was saying was honest and genuine. She was glowing like an electric light bulb, bright, radiant and beaming with an essence. There was more to this lady than being a country singer, I just didn't know what it was!

" There is a wonderful chance coming up for you very soon Lindsy. When it presents itself to you, take it! " Now I was confused, was she a kind of psychic? But deep down inside of me, every particle was telling me she was being truthful.

" In a very short time Lindsy, things beyond your wildest dreams are going to happen. And no! I'm not psychic." Cina let out a quiet soft laugh as she spoke those words. Maybe she could read my mind!?

I started to think where I might have known her from in the past, but nothing came to mind. The overwhelming feeling that I did know her from

somewhere was very strong. If I had been
one of twins, then she would have fitted into that
category.

She looked at me with sparkling eyes still, then
withdrew her hand, explaining she would have to
continue with the concert.

" Here is my email address Lindsy. When the time is
right, and you will know when that is, you
can get in touch so that I can help guide you on your
new path." She raised her body to her feet,
slowly starting to move away from the table.

" Tonight! You have opened your mind to something
you had no idea about, and love has
entered into your life in a way you didn't know was
possible." A bigger smile beamed from her,
then walked a little faster to the stage to join the
other group members.

Again! I was asking myself what just happened?
Static electricity ran through my entire body. I
could have been plugged into the national electrical
grid, but my God it felt good.

Music once again entered the room as more songs
flooded the ears of the party goers.

It was hard to believe that I was listening to every
song, but mainly concentrating on Cina. Every
now and then, she smiled over at me, one time she
winked, it felt so good that a spark of life had
come into my life in a way I couldn't imagine.

From the beginning of the night, until now, a strange
atmosphere had engulfed the dancehall.

Don't get me wrong, I had no clue that strange
things could happen to you like that, but, wow!
What a difference in me from entering those doors to
that very moment. It was good to feel alive
in ways, I had never experienced before.

I am not a religious person, meaning I don't go to

any church, but I always believed there was a spiritual path in my life. A path that sometimes pointed me in directions I didn't dream of going towards. Did I believe in a God? I believed there was something that I chose to call a God, a power so great, I didn't understand. Sometimes, I would get impulses, like sparks, run through my mind and body, then think there was something or someone around me.

I have had wonderful quiet moments in my life. Some were filled with peace and tranquility, others, calm serene moments covered in an unseen bright light. I never spoke of these things to anyone. I guess that was me not wanting to spook people who wouldn't or couldn't understand my thoughts.

What a beautiful night! What a wonderful singer who was singing with the power of love. My eyes had opened wider today. I needed to be grateful for being allowed to feel a warmth and kindness from someone who I didn't know, but felt I was going to get to know quite well.

Arriving back at the apartment around midnight, I started to remove my party clothes, then stepped into the warm running shower water.

I was feeling very refreshed and clean standing brushing my blond hair, untangling the wet strands as the water was dripping.

The electrical sparks I felt earlier that night returned to me as I was looking at my reflection in the long wall mirror. There was a glow about my body, a bright misty light surrounded my skin.

I believe I was witnessing my aura, something I had never seen before.

When Cina Samson came into my life. She lit up my life like a lighthouse beacon.

Somehow I knew things were going to change, and for the better.

I probably fell asleep within ten minutes of my head hitting the pillows. Not in my entire life had I felt as calm and full of peace as I did right then. I remember floating slowly and peacefully into what I thought was another dimension. Floating through clouds of color. The feeling of flying with no wings and no engines attached to me. I was very slowly being guided to a wonderful blazing white light. " Lindsy! Lindsy! " Such a beautiful ladies voice came to the attention of my ears. Her voice was like humming and soft base tones. Like being carried on the unseen wind, her voice faded then returned with the next gust of air. Floating and standing upright, I stood before the dazzling bright light. I wanted so much to enter that pulsating energy before me. I believe that I could have passed through into that light without a second thought, but, as I decided to go forward, appearing in front of me was the most beautiful colored bird, hovering with its wings flapping in slow motion.

The soft tones of the ladies voice returned.

" This creature you see before you Lindsy is a red cardinal. She will help guide you whenever you need help. She will always be there, all you have to do is think of her."

There was something familiar in the ladies voice. I knew I had heard it before, but just couldn't place it in a time, or place.

In all my life, I had never had such a marvelous and deep peaceful sleep as I did that night.

The energy was still around and running through my entire body. I thought back to the wonderful feelings and dreams I had. My eyes flickering towards

the open balcony window. The frilled curtains swaying slightly with a warm breeze.
The balcony railing glistened as the morning sun shon around the building.
I thought back to the bright light in the dream. Vivid colors came into my mind.
" What a beautiful dream that was. " I thought.
" Would be fantastic if it had been real. " I said to myself smiling.
As I focused my eyes on the railing outside, my eyes couldn't believe what they were seeing.
Balancing on the chrome rail was the most radiant red looking bird I had ever seen.
It was the red cardinal standing there. I could have sworn it was smiling at me as I lay there in disbelief.
" Oh my God! The dream was real! And now I remember where I had heard the ladies voice.
It was CINA!..........

Chapter 3
Life and Death

I never was certain how all these wonderful things
came to be, but, boy was I starting to enjoy
incredibly awesome feelings, emotions, and generally
things I just couldn't explain.
Awakening from that first nights sleep after listening
to Cina, then focusing my eyes on the red
Cardinal perched on the balcony rail was tattooed
into my thoughts.
With precision sounds, I remember the musical notes
this country singer sang. It was hypnotizing
also the red cardinal singing that first morning. The
bright fire engine red plumage mixed with a
smooth black around its beak and inside the wings
running the length of the feathers.
I think what stood out the most was its bright almost
smiling eyes. What was the significance of
all this? I had the strangest feeling I was about to
find out on a daily basis.
My mind, my entire body, every nerve ending, was
coming to life.
With the warm shower water cascading over and on
my naked body, I felt so alive, every touch
of my hands on my skin sent electrical pulses the
entire length of my torso, from the tips of my
toes to the blond hair strands on my head.
Reaching for a large bathrobe I gently dried the
water droplets from my body.
" What the hell!? " I lost my balance slightly before
grabbing the shower rail to prevent me from
falling.
At this point, I thought I was going crazy, what I was
staring at was a silhouette of a small

young girl. She was standing in the full-length mirror before me. She couldn't have been more
than Twelve years old. I could make out the rough outline of her body, her face looked pale and
unwell. As I looked in the mirror and what I was gazing at, she moved her right hand up to the
glass then pointed her finger on to the steamed up mirror.

" SAVE ME! PLEASE SAVE ME!" She asked in a frightened voice. The voice sounded so
distant, like someone pleading for help the voice trembled as the sounds got farther away, then
silence.

With the silhouette fading as quickly as it appeared, I stood there with my mouth wide open as to
what just happened. Was I scared? I think if I had a heart condition, It would have missed beats
or stopped!

Sitting down with my soaking wet butt on a shower stool, I was trying to shake myself back into
reality.

A very soothing moment washed over me as I sat drinking a strong mug of coffee. As frightening
for a moment that was, I began to believe that this apparition meant me no harm. But, What was
she coming to me for? Who was she? Hopefully, the answers would present themselves soon.

Finishing my coffee and standing on the balcony I looked down at the metal rail where the red
cardinal had been perched.

The earlier encounter with the young girl was still fixed in my mind. In less than twenty-four
hours, my life had been totally turned around. Weird things were coming at me from all
directions. I drank the last drops of coffee as I

glanced at my watch. " OMG! I need to move fast to get to work on time!" I grabbed my jacket running towards the apartment front door.

" Lindsy! You are on sections one to four today in emergency admissions! Doctor Mike Sanders is a duty on-call junior doctor, be gentle with him!" Said Doctor Adams, the head of staff for that day. He smiled that knowing smile as he knew I could be mischievous around junior Doctors. It's a known fact that behind every Doctor, there's a nurse that helps prevent the patients from being tortured unnecessarily. I smiled to myself thinking those thoughts.

I remember well that morning walking into emergency room two. I was standing at the foot of the bed looking at an eighty-two-year-old lady. She was pale and looked like she was weather worn!. Her arms were very wrinkled with dark blue and purple colored veins. As I adjusted the settings on her EKG machine that was monitoring every heartbeat. Her blood pressure was seriously high.

Checking her Introvenus drip and making sure the needles in her hand was secure, I glanced down towards her eyes. She was half sleepy, her green eyes sparkled in the emergency ward lights. When I looked at her decaying vital signs, my instinct knowingly kicked into action.

Her body and health were just suffering badly from an older age! I had seen so many wonderful human beings come into the emergency rooms, and sadly, some were on their way out of this world.

" Your name is Lindsy! You will be the last person I see before I'm called home. It's a privilege for me to see such a beautiful young angel like you! I always knew that an afterlife exists, but

right now, you standing there confirmed it!" My eyebrows raised slightly with her saying those words, but, I knew that with powerful drugs to lengthen life expectancy, hallucinations occur. Tucking the bed linen so she was warm and as comfortable as possible, I spoke quietly near her ear.

" Have you any relatives on their way here to see you miss Robinson?"

" I have no living relatives Lindsy! But my family is already here standing next to you!" She

smiled back at me with a shiny teardrop running down her cheek.

Trying to reassure her she was going to be fine, she interupted my words.

"It's ok Lindsy! I know I'm in my last few minutes of life in this body. I have had a good life. I'm

ready to go home now." She continued. " You have some wonderful times ahead of you, your

real journey has just begun today. I am to tell you that the red cardinal will never desert you.

Trust in your new path, always look to the stars when you need an answer.

Now its time for me to say goodbye young angel. Live! Love! And laugh!" A long drawn out

breath exhaled from her body.

The alarm buzzed loudly around the emergency room as the EKG machine had now stopped

picking up heartbeats.

" Get out my way you stupid nurse!" came the gruff voice from Doctor Mike Sanders as he

barged pass Lindsy nearly knocking her to the floor. He listened to the woman's chest for signs of life, but he heard nothing as he removed his

Stethoscope.

" Yep! She's gone! Put a toe tag on and bag her up for the morgue!"

I stood behind the Doctor as he wrote down on a scrap piece of paper at the time of death.

In the minute that followed, it was quite a blur. What I remember was going into a blind rage at this poor excuse for a Doctor. A rude disrespectful young guy who had a stone for a heart!

" SLAP!" My right hand caught him side on, his left cheek was bright red as I removed my hand.

" If you ever touch me like that again Doctor, I will press charges for assault. You are one of the rudest, arrogant shits I've ever come across. For the rest of my work today, I suggest you use another nurse to assist you, or you will have a matching hand print on your other cheek!"

Seeing everything, Doctor Adams looked sternly at the junior Doctor. His eyes were furious as he stared at the young intern.

" I will see you in my office right now Doctor! " Said the chief consultant. The young Doctor Looked angry as he glanced at Lindsy walking quickly passed her.

With the office door closed behind both Doctors, the voice of the chief could be heard muffled, no words were distinguishable, but by the loudness and tone of the sounds, he was getting an ass kicking of enormous proportions.

Lindsy was usually an easy going type of woman, but one thing she always hated was disrespect for another person. This older lady even though deceased, still deserved that respect.

Lindsy thought back to the older lady. Was she that delirious that she thought she saw an angel

before her? With all the latest crazy things going on in the last day, maybe she just saw Lindsy's
bright aura that even she thought she could see now. Doctor Adams sat next to Lindsy placing his lunch tray on the table.

" Are you ok?" He asked in a concerned voice, then continued.

" I have suspended Doctor Sanders for two weeks, Lindsy! That will take him up to the
beginning of your vacation. So you won't need to work with him for five weeks. If he doesn't
improve in that time, I will run his butt out of this hospital so fast, his feet will be on fire."

" I mean him no harm Doctor, but if that's going to be fully qualified after his final probationary
period, then I pity his patients, and staff who need to work with him." Lindsy looked down at her
food stirring the tomatoes into her salad.

" You are one of the most caring nurses I know young lady! You dedicate your self to the
Patience and help wherever possible with the other staff. There is no one more suited to this job
than you! All the board of directors and Doctors have noticed you big time, Lindsy! You could
have been a Doctor yourself if you had put your mind to it!" Lindsy started to blush with all the
kind words he was speaking.

" I watch all the good work you do in the hospital Doctor. I admire all the dedication each one of
you gives back into this place! Saving lives, reassuring relatives that everything possible is being
done to help their loved ones. I have shed many tears when you see the wonderful smiles on the
patient's faces when you tell them everything is working out fine!"

" I love what I do Lindsy! I have a genuine

satisfaction when I see I've made a slight difference in someone's life!" He said proudly.

Doctor Adams could be a bit of a joker himself at times, so when he picked up the cream-filled cake, removed the cherry top, then gently lifted the cake up and squashed a little of the cream on her nose. With his other hand, then placed the cherry on the creamy nose.

He gave out a shallow laugh, winked at her and said. " Now you feel better right!? " Lindsy with her eyes wide open looked surprised, then burst into laughter saying back to him.

" And you are forty-three going on ten?" Wiping the cream off and then placed the cherry in her petite mouth. " Glad you're feeling better, now get your cute butt back to work" Winking at her for a second time.

" I'm going to give you some more morphine Mr. Anderson. This should help to relieve the pain in your leg!" Lindsy said to one of the latest admissions. The new patient had been working on a cutting tool on his farm. After several minutes one of the heavy metal bolts on the machinery sheered off and sent the cutting blade speeding down towards his leg, then embedded in the upper thigh. Lindsy knew from past experience that he was probably going to lose his leg. But she kept a caring and wonderful smile on her face as she administered the strong painkilling drug.

" How does that feel now Mr. Anderson?" She asked in a sincere voice.

" Wow! I feel like I'm floating in clouds, and hardly feel anything in my leg now, so thank you Nurse." He replied with a type of drunk look on his face.

Lindsy knew that morphine can give you the drunk feeling. She also knew that he could not feel any other part of his leg because of the cutting tool embedded deep inside the skin and slicing the bone slightly when it dug in through his skin. Doctor Adams slowly walked into the emergency room holding a clipboard and a chart attached to it. " There's no easy way of telling you this Mr. Anderson. I always find it better to tell the patients the truth, most people respect that! It's not easy to swallow not good news, but I believe you are strong and will accept the news with a brave attitude." The Doctors face was sincere and concerned all at the same time.

" I know what you are going to say, Doctor, I think I knew when I see the damage the blade has done. If the leg needs to be cut off to save my life, then that's what needs to happen." He smiled still high on the powerful morphine.

" Good man! You will need to go into theater straight away, the operating staff is prepping now as we speak. Have you got relatives here or coming in?" The Doctor asked.

" My wife is driving from Göteborg and left about ten minutes ago."

" Good!" Said the Doctor. " We will tell her everything that's going on while you are in the operating room, so try not to worry. Someone will keep her informed all the time. You are in the hands of a very skilled surgeon and nursing staff." Doctor Adams said holding the man's hand and gently tapping it to reassure him. At that moment, two other male nurses came in and organized the patient to transfer him to the theater. Lindsy smiled at him as he was wheeled out on the hospital emergency stretcher.

As always at times, no sooner had they seen to the patient, another alarm sounded from the Doctors and nursing station.

" There's an ambulance on its way here. ETA three minutes! Young child thirteen years old, Shes had her heart started twice in the vehicle. All none active personnel to the emergency room four now, please." The message was relayed to the speaker system throughout the whole emergency area.

With the emergency doors from the ambulance parking area sliding open. Two paramedics ran with the young girl on the portable stretcher.

" Get her on the emergency bed now!" Shouted Doctor Adams. All staff in the room knew exactly what to do as each one prepared syringes and wires to be attached to the now lifeless body.

" Get that defibrillator charged up now! "He stated in an agitated voice. "Her heart has stopped again."

The defibrillator crackled and the sound of an increasing tone from low to high volume reached all the medical team around her.

" STAND CLEAR! STAND CLEAR!" Came the electronically synthesized voice.

A loud thump could be heard with a clicking noise at the end of the discharge from the Defibrillator. It immediately started to charge again as the Doctor listened for sounds of her heart. The young girls back arched from the bed as the electric current raced through her entire body. Her skin color was a deep white and gave the impression she was anemic.

" STAND CLEAR! STAND CLEAR!" Repeated the machine. Everyone stood back as the
Doctor placed the paddles on the girl's chest for the second time.
Again came the arched back on the child and the thump sound echoing around the emergency
Room.
Only seconds past with everything been done to try and save this young girls life.
Listening for any signs of life, the Doctor removed his stethoscope, this time slowly. The
expression he had was written all over his face. A sadness was witnessed as he started to look at
his watch.
" What a damn shame for someone so young! Time of death! 15.42. When her parents arrive,
show them into my office straight away, please!"
All the emergency staff was empty of any smiles. The rooms clock could be heard ticking away
making everyone aware that time still marched forward.
I loved being a nurse, however, times like this did happen. Sometimes it would cause a numb
sensation, then mixed with a disbelief.
Being the only staff member in the room, I closed the door for preparing the girl for
transportation to the morgue. Very slowly I started to remove all the wires and drips from the
now lifeless body.
I lifted the white bed sheet from the base of the bed, then gently pulled it upwards to cover the
entire body. I was secretly hoping that her parents wouldn't walk in while I was preparing her
young body.
Just as the sheet reached her head, I jumped back still holding the sheet tightly in my hands.

" No way! Oh my god!" Lindsy shouted to an empty room.

She stood there riveted to the floor in disbelief. Before her, the young girls face could be seen clearly with her eyes. In all the quickness of the emergency, Lindsy had not seen her face.

Very few seconds had passed by, then she had thoughts running through her mind as the memory kicked into motion of the apparition in her bathroom mirror. It was the same face and child that had asked to save her. The next thoughts were how could she help this girl now she was dead?

Lindsy began to get very emotional as she felt powerless to do anything standing in front of the emergency bed. She crouched down towards the floor not knowing and what she could still do or have done to help the girl.

Magic can reveal itself in many ways and at that precise moment, something very magical happened. Perched on the metal headboard was the red cardinal! This time, there was a transparency about it, like it was a form of mist or ghostly looking.

" I see you cardinal, but what can I do now to help her? Shes already gone!" Lindsy anxiously asked the unexpected creature.

Like a movie being planted in her mind, she was very aware of developing moving pictures on a white screen in her thoughts.

Again with disbelief, Lindsy witnessed the developing pictures focus and saw that it was her standing next to the girl as she lay there motionless. She continued to see herself place her hands on the girl's naked chest.

The girl felt cold as she watched herself rest her hands over where her heart would be deep inside her body.

Without hesitating, Lindsy duplicated what she saw in the vision. The young girl's skin was cold to the touch.

It was probably less than ten seconds when Lindsy started to feel something. The way to describe what she felt, was like crackles of sparks from a campfire. As she looked at her hands, she could have sworn her own skin was glowing in her palms. She was right!

Between her hands and the cold skin, an orange, yellow light glowed. The light started to lift Lindsy's hands within a few inches of the body. Both hands began to float over the girl like a hovercraft. Very small circular movements could be seen.

The red cardinal who had been overseeing everything flew and then hovered above Lindsy's right hand. Red! Black! Orange and Yellow blended together mixed like an artists paint pallet as the Cardinals transparent body joined with her hands and every single color present.

The bird's wings flapped and encompassed both her hands conjuring up some kind of sparkling Bright circular force field. It shon so brightly as the sounds crackled and hummed. Small minature lightening streaks shot down to the girl's chest penetrating deep into her body.

Lindsy became very calm and relaxed as the unknown energies left her hands. Whatever was happening was leaving a peaceful beautiful residue throughout her entire body.

Lindsy felt that she was in two places at once. Standing over the girl was one, the other, seeing herself on the white screen in her mind. The image was like someone was filming her and she saw everything from a different angle. What she was experiencing more than anything, was the feeling of one hundred percent love.

Seconds! Not minutes passed with the beat of her own heart. On the screen in her mind, a white radiant straight beam of light shot from her own body directly to the young girl's chest.

Flashing pulses of light lit up the emergency room like a Christmas tree. Then! Darkness.

Absolute darkness!

A very fine pinpoint of light could be seen from Lindsys eyes. The light was a small bright white light. Growing in size and brightness, she was beginning to focus on what she was looking at.

The ceiling of the emergency room came into view. She was laying on the cold floor looking at that and the smiling Doctor Adams.

I've got you, Lindsy! You're ok now" He said with an unbelievable smile that was strange for her, as a death had just occurred.

Shaking her head a few times, she focused on more of the room. She realized that at least five staff were around her, and as she looked up at the young girls emergency bed, the EKG machine and all the drips were re-connected to her!

My eyes were bulging twice the size as normal as I glanced at the now opened eyed young Sarah Berg!

" She's alive!!!" I shouted stumbling to my feet. Doctor Adams told one of the other nurses to take me into his office, and he would be in as soon as he had completed a full examination of Sarah. Closing his office door behind him, he turned to look at me with a smile and a raised eyebrow.

" Now young lady! Would you like to tell me what

happened in there?" He asked in a quiet
toned voice. I thought for a moment. With a focus on
how the hell I was going to explain
something that I didn't even know what had
happened.
Doctor Adams continued as he pulled his office chair
out from the desk, then sat down.
" All the emergency staff witnessed bright colored
lights coming from the girl's room. After
hearing the thud of someone falling on the floor, we
all ran in and discovered the girl alive and
you lying unconscious. I can only say that something
miraculous has happened, But what?"
" I think if I tell you exactly what happened Doctor
Adams, you will be reaching for the desk
phone and calling the Psychiatric unit to come and
look after me!"
" In all my years of being a Doctor, Lindsy, I always
tried to keep an open mind! I do know
though that some kind of miracle has happened, and
you definitely had something to do with it!"
I always remember the Doctors face when I explained
all the crazy things that had started to
happen from being at the country and western night
to the blackout I suffered just minutes ago.
Both of his eyebrows had risen higher on his head
now, and then within a few seconds, lowered
with a confused smile as he sat back more in his
chair.
" I knew I had to try something, I was given the
vision for a reason. Now I see that something
that we would say was, and is impossible, became
real! I'm just as confused as you are. But, my
God! Shes alive Doctor!" The Doctor shuffled a little in
his seat.
" Her vital signs are exceptional. She has signs of

being one of the healthiest humans on the
planet. There is no sign of heart problems, her blood
pressure is perfect! She wants to speak to
you, Lindsy! You can do that shortly, the nursing
staff is talking to her parents as we speak."
" I feel so alive myself Doctor! I also feel totally
different, for the better of course! Everything
since I woke up on the floor is more in tune with me
than ever in my life! I have tapped into
 something wonderful, I feel like I'm being guided to
do fantastic and maybe unexplained
things."
The Doctor smiled yet again, only this time, a warm
glow extended from his face. It didn't
matter what had happened, the girl was living and
breathing. She was diagnosed dead not so long
ago, now she was a living miracle.
Collecting her thoughts, then wiping away any floor
dust from her nursing uniform, she walked
towards the emergency room where Sarah lay.
On either side of the bed, the young girl's Mother and
Father held a hand each. Smiling and tears
ran down their faces, all eyes reflecting the rooms
bright lights.
" You saved our daughter, nurse!" Said the girls
Mother. She continued.
" When Sarah told us the other day that a nurse
called Lindsy will save her life, we thought she
was just delusional and high with a fever. But here
we are right now witnessing something that
may only happen probably once in a lifetime!" The
girl's Mother wiped her tears from both eyes.
She continued.
" We will always be in your debt, Lindsy! You
somehow through the grace of God gave us back
our daughter. Keep our home and cell phone

numbers safe, and anytime we might be able to help you, don't hesitate to ask if it's in our power to assist you in any way."

The Mother, Chantell Berg, reached into her purse and began scribbling their telephone numbers on a notepad, then, tore off the single sheet of paper and handed it to Lindsy.

" Thank you so much, Mrs. Berg, but, I'm only doing my job here in the hospital. It's a pleasure to have been able to do something good for Sarah, even though I'm not sure what just happened."

Sarahs Father stood up from the chair, then walked over slowly to Lindsy.

Placing both arms around Lindsy, he pulled her closer to his own body, then put one hand on the back of her head. " You have a New path to follow Lindsy!" He said.

" For whatever purpose, God, as you do or don't understand him, has chosen you to do wonderful work. Listen to your heart, Lindsy! Today, you saved a little girl, tomorrow? Well, tomorrow who knows what miracles you will be able to achieve." He released his hold on her, then went to sit back down next to Sarah.

Sarah whispered to her Mothers ear. Chantell looked at Tom, her husband. "Let's go to the canteen area and get a well-deserved coffee, darling!" She said wiping the remaining tears from her face, but with a wide smile replacing the traumatic wrinkles that had occurred.

The now empty emergency room. Except for Sarah and Lindsy staring at each other.

Sarah had a beautiful smile on her face. The room lit up with the glow from her now bright pink cheeks. Sarah stretched her hand out to the happy but slightly confused Lindsy.

" I knew you could save me, Lindsy! I had my guardian angel standing next to me when I saw you in my dream. He said, " Here is your earth angel, Sarah! She will help save your life. Reach out to her from your mind and she will hear you!"

" Oh! I certainly heard you, Sarah!" Lindsy replied chuckling quietly, then continued.

" You scared the hell out of me for a few seconds, but then I knew you meant me no harm."

Lindsy had sat down next to the young girl.

" I know that I am young, and I also know now that I have a great life in front of me. Thanks To you!" All the time she spoke, Sarah had held tightly Lindsy's hand.

" Did you know that your heart had stopped working Sarah? Were you scared?" Lindsy asked with a curious mind.

" Most of the time, I felt very safe. My guardian angel said. " I had a choice." He told me I could go with him, or ask for your help! I wanted so much to grow up and have children, and find someone who would fall in love with me." Sarah had a bigger smile when she said that, then continued. " I just wanted so much to live and be with Mom and Dad."

" Well now you have that chance young lady, you are going to do great things. When the time is right, you will have children of your own. That special person will come into your life when you're ready." Lindsy held her hand with a gentleness, she was full of happiness as the girl got to live.

In the daily routines of the emergencies, today was a day in this room that in death, it became life. ....

Chapter 4
Staten Island

In the time from meeting Sarah and her parents, nothing unusual had happened. There was an excitement around Lindsy now. Today she was flying away on her much-needed vacation.

New York, New York. Just to unwind and chill for a while was really pleasing to Lindsy.

Being the first time in the States, she wanted to see as much of the city as she could. Three weeks was ample time to have as much fun as she could fit in.

" Ladies and Gentlemen! This is your captain speaking. My name is Captain Mark Andrews. I along with my co-pilot James Lincoln will be flying at an altitude of thirty-eight thousand feet. Our journey time will be approximately six and a half hours, we should arrive at John F Kennedy Airport seven PM local time. Please take notice of any overhead signs and do ask our flight attendants if you have any questions or need snacks or beverages. On behalf of the crew and my self, thank you for flying Pan-Atlantic Airlines."

Lindsy sat back in the first-class seat. Having waited a while for a well-needed rest, she splashed out extra for the comfort. Personal headphones, ten-inch in-flight tv monitor, and last but not least, a fully reclinable seat that turned into a bed. The aircraft was three-quarters full with people from many different countries. Many were middle-aged businessmen returning to the states. Her younger age made her stand out from the crowd, and with a gentle smile now shining, she began to relax and took a sip of the dark vodka and coke in front of her.

Reflecting back on the previous week's adventures, she mulled over all the crazy things that had happened. From first meeting Cina, and then the dream, the red cardinal, and seeing the young girl Sarah in her mirror before helping somehow to save her life. Was she really chosen for something out of the ordinary? Her thoughts gently ran from side to side in her head. From the emergency room with Sarah, Lindsy felt so alive. Her instincts were becoming sharper, like being fine-tuned into an unseen force. There was definitely more to this world and life than she knew.

" If there's anything I can get you, madam, please don't hesitate to use the steward call button. An extra pillow if you need to rest. " A very handsome flight attendant smiled at Lindsy, then moved forward to the next passengers in front of her. The window seat she had acquired was situated near the front of the plane and she could see the lower cloud ceiling beneath the aircraft. Lindsy was beginning to be very relaxed and calmness ascended upon her.

Gaps in the cloud formations allowed her to see patches of land thousands of feet below.

Today was the beginning of a special time for her to explore this wonderful world.

Of course, it would have been wonderful to have had that missing special person in her life at that moment, but deep down inside her now calmed mind, she somehow knew that he was going to turn up when the powers that be decided, who or whatever the powers that be, were.

"So, you see now why I'm writing down my story.

From that first day, my life changed. I guess
that my life had even from the day I was born, was
set down on a human life map somewhere in
this vast universe. It had taken thirty years for me to
begin to awaken, but wow! Boy was I
waking up fast."

Lindsy sat back in her apartment comfortable
computer chair pondering on how to continue in
her private diary.

The world wide web was a massive space of Mega
and Gigabytes. It contained billions of data
from billions of people, floating in cyberspace. This
hidden place contained many secrets,
writing in a secret diary was probably the best thing
to do. Things like the events happening to
her could be used against her, so she wasn't going to
divulge that information for some
intelligent computer hacker to discover something
that could be described as impossible and
fantasy.

Leaning slightly forward again, she picked up the
dark blue ballpoint pen, then continued to
write.

" Returning back to that day on the flight to the
states, I had that uneasy feeling in the pit of my
stomach. I knew some kind of weird was just about
to happen. Then it did, In quite a scary way."

" Ladies and gentlemen! This is your captain
speaking. Is there a doctor or any medical nurses on
board today? We have an emergency in the rear
section of the plane. Please make your self-
known to the flight crew!" The captain's voice was
concerned.

" I immediately beckoned to the male flight
attendant. He quickly came to my seat and enquired
if it was to do with the medical emergency?"

" I'm a nurse, can I be of help?" He nodded to me and quietly whispered in my ear.
" We think a middle-aged man is having a heart attack, he's complaining of severe chest pains and his color is very pale white."
Lindsy didn't need to think twice, and shot to her feet fast and began to follow the steward along the middle gangway.
As she walked at a very quick pace towards the rear of the plane, she tried to compose herself and began thinking about how to best deal with the patient.
Unknown to the male steward and Lindsy, a man was kneeling down next to the aircraft floor alongside the middle-aged man.
Arriving at the man laying on the floor, Lindsy said to the second flight attendant and the man kneeling.
" Hey! My name is Lindsy. I'm a nurse." Lindsy reached down and started to roll the mans left shirt sleeve so she could feel for his pulse.
" Hi, Lindsy! I am Doctor Amire Sharf. I believe we had a heart attack condition here. With limited medical supplies with me, we need to get him stabilized as best we can!" The thirty-plus looking Doctor replied, then continued.
The cabin crew went quickly to get the onboard defibrillator in case it was needed. One of the stewards returned and started to remove the machine from its case.
" I am going to give you a shot of nitro spray John." He said looking directly at the sick man.
John Palmer was heading back to America after vacationing in Europe. The middle-aged guy was a little overweight, this could have contributed to his present condition

" This spray is very powerful and could lower your blood pressure severely, but we are going to keep a close eye on you. You have an experienced Doctor and a beautiful young nurse assisting me! You're going to be fine John." Amire gently Patted the man's arm and smiled down at him.

" Lindsy! Can you." The young Doctor stopped in mid-sentence. He was staring directly at her bright sparkling eyes. For a moment, she was still concentrating on John. When Amire had failed to continue the words, she raised her head slowly. An electrifying connection between two pairs of eyes was taking place. In her mind. The thoughts were. " Oh my God! You're the one I've been looking for all my life."

There were two underlying smiles as they fixed their gaze on each other.

In both male and female bodies, some kind of magnetic handcuffs enveloped the two beating hearts. Each second of their stare made the hearts fluctuate rapidly. In all the previous years in her life, she never had tingling sensations in her virginal area when just looking at a man, but, today, an explosion of fireworks was taking place in her underwear.

She could feel her face get warmer, she knew her cheeks had turned blush red!

Thoughts hurried again through her mind. If she was joined by skin to his body, she couldn't have felt closer to this complete stranger than she did at that moment. A moment that sent mixed emotional feelings cascading throughout her entire being. If she didn't know any better, she could have sworn she just had an orgasm, and not even touching him. This was incredible. No man ever had made her feel like this. She wasn't complaining, she just for only seconds, was enjoying the beautiful rush and feelings throughout her physical and emotional state.

Amire looked away from Lindsy, then directed his attention to Daniela, the flight stewardess.

" Daniela! Can you tell the captain? In my opinion, this passenger has had a severe heart attack! We need to get him to the nearest emergency hospital! We also need oxygen to help with his breathing." Without hesitating, the stewardess ran the few meters to the cabin crews telephone, this was a direct line to the captain in the cockpit.

" Captain, sir! We have a doctor and nurse with the passenger now. They are treating him for a heart attack! The doctor says " We need to get to the nearest airport and emergency hospital!"

There were a few seconds where silence remained on the phone handset.

" Daniela! We are only about two hours from New York! I can increase our speed a little and give you an approximate ETA of ninety minutes." She went to replace the handset, then quickly placed it back to her ear.

" Oh! One more thing sir. The Doctor needs oxygen for the patient. Permission to deploy the emergency oxygen tank?"

" Of course Daniela!" She thanked the captain and hung the receiver back on the hook.

Without even thinking. Lindsy placed her left hand on the mans bare chest. Now thoughts started flooding into her mind. Could she work another kind of miracle like the young girl? In that moment of thought, she once again felt the electrical energies pulsating through her arm and fingers.

" I think his heart is quite strong, Lindsy!" The young

Doctor stared back at her bright eyes.
He was mesmerized. He looked like a lonely lost
puppy dog! Every few seconds, he tried to look
away from her so he could concentrate on the
patient. But then the magnetic pull from her gaze
made him turn to her once, then again. His heart was
pounding probably like Johns, and his
heart was in perfect condition. In good health, but
beating hard at what beauty he was staring at.
With every passing second, both of them had not
noticed Lindsy's hand starting to glow from her
hand palm. Amire had moved his eyes towards the
stewardesses face that had caught his
attention. Her eyes had begun to bulge slightly, and
then her mouth dropped open more.
In the direction of the stewardesses gaze, he
followed the look to Johns' chest. Startled! He
inhaled a quick intake of air into his lungs.
Right before the stewardess, Amire, and Lindsy was
the most amazing pulsating orange glow
jetting from her hand. It was lighting up the area
around them like a multi bulbed Christmas tree.
In an instant, Amire found himself placing his right
hand on top of hers. Her hand was drawing
his skin to hers. Suddenly! His fingers felt like they
were fused together like a piece of metal to a
soldering task. Small fluorescent blue sparks ignited
their hands. The next moment, like
lightning streaks from the clouds, the bolts forced
their way into Johns' chest. No burns could be
seen. Each strike of the bolts of light gently
penetrated the mans body. There was now a gentle
smile on Johns' face. He looked at peace, and more
comfortable.
" Is it some kind of new medical device Lindsy?"
Asked the flight attendant.

" You could say that!" Replied the secretive Lindsy.
Amire smiled at Lindsy, he didn't take his eyes off her
for a second. She was becoming a kind of
drug to him. If he removed his gaze from her even
for a moment, the overwhelming urge to look
back was incredible. With each minute passing, an
unseen energy was emerging between John,
Amire, and Lindsy. Even the stewardess was
beginning to feel something wonderful with all the
glowing light. If each one were to describe at that
moment what they felt, then all four of them
would say. " I can feel so much unseen love! I can't
see it, but my heart does! I never want this
feeling to go away."
Seconds turned in to minutes, each minute gave John
an abundance of electrical impulses, not
just him, but all four of them.
As the particle charged air circled around them all,
the scene was being relayed to somewhere in
the universe. Each one of the four, feeling that loving
eyes were watching every single move
they made.
Emotional confusion entered each one of them,
including the stewardess. Each, in turn, could
feel something so powerful, but so wonderful.
On the face of John, he looked like he had some kind
of spiritual encounter. The truth was,
actually, he did! For him personally, it would be a few
years until he realized what had taken
place. He would then understand completely what
and why he was taken ill on that flight.
Lindsy began to move away from John. She became
aware that the lights from her hands were
now fading. Sitting back sideways on the seat, she
continued to look down at her hands, then
rubbed them gently together which she felt inclined

to do, she could feel the new energies
disbursing into the air around them. What remained
in her mind, body, and soul was a gift. A gift
of serenity, an unseen powerful love.
She felt ten feet tall. She knew that John was going
to make it, someone or something told her
everything was going to be ok!
Amire began to relax a little too, he sat back on his
seat too, still staring at Lindsy, then looking
down to Johns serine face, he was peaceful and a
heart rate that was settling down to a nearly
normal rhythm.
The stewardess brought another pillow for the
patient, she gently propped it under his head.
" Let me say to all three of you. Thank you so much
for giving me a chance to live. What I'm
feeling right now is a perfect peace I've never
experienced before." He said with a glowing smile
aimed at all of them. At the same time reaching for
one of Lindsy's hands and then Amires.
Including the stewardess, all three smiled back at
him, a reassuring smile each that basically said:
" You're welcome!"
Lindsy sitting directly opposite Amire glanced over in
his direction, she too didn't want to
remove her gaze. The ecstatic emotions traveling
through her mind and body was incredible.
" I have a distinct feeling I've met you before Lindsy!
But, I know that's not possible. I feel like
we have somewhere in this vast universe spoken
before." He said still smiling at the beautiful
person in front of him.
If anything, this flight was full of contagious smiles,
also an unseen energy that wrapped around
each of their souls.
" I feel something, similar Doctor! There is an

underlying feeling of Deja Vous! Like I've been here in this exact situation. A curious memory like a video recording of this scene." Still looking at him with a pair of love filled eyes. She continued.
" In my earlier years at school, I had lessons in many different subjects, and one, in particular, was that of magnets. When I watched two black magnets clang together at lightning speed, then stuck fast and was like the effect of super glue had on materials. I have that strange feeling right now with you!" At that moment, she went bright red on both cheeks, then said.
" Oh my God! Did I say that out loud!?" She gave a little laugh and covered her face with both hands.
Amire had a beaming smile, his eyes began to glisten, It was almost like no-one had ever said anything as nice to him in his entire life.
" I think the two of you should get a room." Came a low toned voice from the patient laying on the cabin floor. Each one of them laughed loudly, some passengers nearby were curious as to why a medical emergency was creating laughter? Perfectly normal reaction from them, but, they would never know what had been going on.
" I would like to give you my cell number Lindsy. Maybe we can meet up for coffee in New York before you go back to Sweden?" He said excitedly.
" Oh I think that might be possible, I will let you know towards the end of my first week." She replied.
Interrupting their conversation, the public address system crackled into life from the planes speakers.
" Ladies and gentlemen! This is the captain again! We

would like to let you know that
a medical emergency has been dealt with by two
wonderful passengers! The patient is
comfortable, and extra good news is, a good tailwind
has enabled us to be one hour five minutes
ahead of schedule. We have been cleared to land on
an emergency runway, and medical teams
will be on standby on the ground to transfer the
patient to a New York hospital by helicopter.
On behalf of the airline, we would like to thank so
much, Doctor Amire, and nurse Lindsy for
their invaluable help in this situation."
Rapturous applause came from the entire aircraft, the
sound even exceeded the plane jet engines.
Some passengers shouted " Hooray!" Like someone
was celebrating a birthday or anniversary.
The captain once again addressed the passengers.
" Please return to your seats, fasten your seatbelts,
when we land, remain seated until we come to
a complete stop. Allow ground medical staff to
evacuate the patient before using the runway
plane steps. Airport busses will be present to take
you to the arrival terminal where shortly after
you will collect your luggage!" The tone of the
captain's voice gave out a sense of relief and
gratitude.
The stewardess started to speak to Amire and Lindsy.
"It's quite alright to stay in these seats, but fasten
your safety belts, I will place the
emergency floor belts around John!" They all nodded
to agree on the request from the
stewardess.
Looking over at Lindsy, Amire knew he had to have a
quick conversation on the incredible
power he witnessed on John.
" How long have you known about your special gifts,

Lindsy?" He asked.

" I was hoping I didn't need to explain myself Amire, but, it's a little late for that now, so, the truth is just a couple of weeks." Lindsy summed it up for him in about four minutes, just before the plane was due to touch down. She continued.

" So you see, whatever this gift I have is, I'm still coming to terms with it. Still being a bit confused and thinking this sort of thing only happens in books or movies, its difficult to comprehend what has happened to me." She replied to him, then looked down to see that John was still peaceful and half sleeping.

Lindsy then had a surprised look on her face as Amire said.

" I've known about mine for about three months now, but my spiritual awakening came along with a ghostly wolf! He was pure white with eyes that would sparkle like stars in the sky.

He started to appear to me when the special healing energies were needed, and strange as this all was to me, I felt privileged to have this wonderful gift. I have read stories about other people who have had similar experiences, but I dismissed them as science fiction, but, here we are both having the same sort of beautiful un-explained forces work with us!

So imagine my surprise when I saw you with glowing light emanating from your hand palms, a pleasant surprise though. Now I know I'm not crazy, but best of all, I'm not alone!"

His face was a picture of happiness, it also gave out a signal that he was so grateful for being in her company.

" Please don't forget to get in touch, Lindsy! If it's not possible for us to meet up, then maybe in the future we can keep in contact through social media, etc!" He said with a slight sadness written over his face.

Lindsy's smile quickly went away at the very thought of not being able to see this beautiful man. This sensual sexy male form, and eyes that would have lit up any bedroom.

" Amire! I need to tell you that my heart is telling me something good is going to happen to you and me! Almost like discovering a special kind of friendship, a feeling from my heart that
 says
you are maybe my long lost soulmate. If I turned away from this brief encounter right now, I know in my very soul that I would have a lifelong regret. I have never spoken to any man like I've spoken to you right now! If truth be told, for what its worth, I'm going to miss you. Does that sound crazy?" She asked with her eyes glistening with tears growing around her pupils.

Amire smiled that beautiful male sexy smile, reached over John to grab her hand, then, gently rubbing the top of her fingers, gripping them a little tighter, then spoke again.

" In my entire life, I have been searching for that special something, and, right now, I don't need to look any further. If someone had told me I would be feeling so wonderful by the time I reached New York on this flight, I wouldn't have believed them! Do I believe in fate? Destiny? Maybe! All I know and feel is that I want to be by your side in the near future." You could tell that every word he spoke, Lindsy knew within her heart, he was feeling the same electric connection.

Lindsy once again brought her mind back into the apartment living room.
Placing the pen on the dining room table, she walked the short distance to the coffee percolator.
The warm black liquid poured slowly into her mug.
She gathered her thoughts and reminisced
about her first encounter with Amire. Fate was
certainly guiding her on a path she knew nothing
of, but, what a beautiful path this was turning out to be.
Returning to her diary she lifted the pen once again, sat comfortably in her computer chair, began
to read back the last few pages, smiled to herself, then put pen to paper to continue her story.
" At this point! Dear reader, you may have decided that everything I've spoken of is untrue!
Believe me! I swear on my mother's life this has been so real!" She wrote, to start where she had
left off.
Her mind drifted back to that beautiful day.

If time had ever stood still, then it was on that flight.
It was like something out of a romance
novel, but with a beautiful twist in how they discovered each other.
Lindsy was very emotional as John was ushered on a paramedic stretcher, then taken to the
waiting helicopter a few meters away.
Standing at the door gangway, Amire and Lindsy looked, then waved at John as he was placed in
the other aircraft.
Before the helicopter doors were closed, they both heard the voice of John as he shouted with a
huge smile over his face.
" You two still need to get a room! And soon!" They chuckled to each other as the helos engines

roared into life.

Passengers were beginning to alight the aircraft with their hand baggage in hand, most were being directed to the center aircraft doors.

" Can you just hold on a few moments?" Asked the stewardess.

Lindsy nodded, and Amire answered with a "Yes! Of course!"

Coming towards them from the front of the aircraft was the beaming, smiling captain.

" What an honor for me to meet two obliging passengers, a doctor, and a nurse. You handled the situation better than any simulation could have achieved!" He said, then continued.

" I have been in contact with the airline head office, they agree with me that you two deserve something special for your invaluable help in this emergency." He reached forward with two envelopes. Handing one each to Amire and Lindsy, he started to explain what the contents were.

" On behalf of myself, Captain Mark Andrews, and Pan-Atlantic airlines, we graciously give you this letter each which entitles you both to unlimited flights for the next five years! Also!

Anytime you are in New York, you can have a five-star hotel of your choice to remind you how much we appreciate your help in saving the other passengers life! All you need to do is call the number inside, and flights and hotels will be booked straight away for you." As they both held their envelopes, they looked surprised but truly grateful for the generous gifts.

Writing her memoirs, she opened the desk drawer, slipping out the white envelope she had been given by the captain.

Thinking deeply as she stared at the short letter, she
smiled to herself, then started to choke up
with emotion as she started to continue her
wonderful memories of that vacation.

" As I continue to tell you of these crazy beautiful
events, I know it all seems incredible. It is!
These types of things don't happen to me, but, they
happened, and continued to happen, time and
time again."

The captain, in turn, shook each of their hands, then
turned to walk back towards the cockpit.
" It's a pleasure for us to have you on this plane, and
maybe one day, we will see each other
again. Thank you!" He glanced back at the two
smiling, Doctor and nurse as he finished his
sentence.
Simultaneously, they both said. " Thank you,
Captain!" They couldn't have synchronized it any
better, like they had rehearsed it for a royal
performance gratitude speech.
Walking through the automatic sliding doors that lead
to the arrival lounge, both of them were
shocked as crowds of people from the flight clapped
loudly. Loud cheering as they both blushed
 walking past them. It was more shocking when just
ahead of them was a TV news crew with
cameras directed in their direction.
" Doctor Amire, Nurse Lindsy! Can we ask you a few
questions as to what happened on the
Plane today?" The news reporter asked.
The investigative journalist continued.
" We heard that the two of you saved a mans life at
thirty-eight thousand feet, Is that true? "
Both Lindsy and Amire could hardly move as the

crowd surged forward, pushing the reporter
and cameraman closer, it was impossible to move
now, so the two had no option but to give out
some kind of statement.
Doctor Amire held on to the tv crews microphone and
leaned forward to talk into it.
" Nurse Lindsy and I were able to treat and stabilize a
heart attack patient, we have just seen him
being airlifted by helicopter to a nearby hospital, but
we believe this man will make a full
recovery. After some medical treatment we
administered to him, he showed great signs of
stabilizing."
" A few of the passengers said they saw an orange
type glow coming from the back of the plane,
was this some new kind of machine you had?" The
reporter asked.
" I think what they might have seen was just a bright
medical torch, they come in handy in
emergency situations. Anyway! We both need to
continue on with our travel, but a special shout
out to the captain and crew for first class service, and
also for the emergency services here at
JFK airport. Must go now! Goodbye!" Amire put his
arm around Lindsys back and tried to usher
her out of the crowded area and tv crew.
" Hopefully, this will be just a five-minute thing,
Lindsy! Should blow over soon." He said,
knowing that what he told the reporter was false,
but, who would believe their story? No one was
going to know about it at this time.
" I have the sneakiest feeling that this isn't going to
be the last we hear about this Amire! My
sixth sense tells me otherwise!" She smiled at him as
they walked quickly through to the airport
exit.

" Taxi!" Amire shouted to the front taxi-cab a few meters away.

Placing his new friend's luggage into the trunk of the vehicle, he opened the rear door for her to
jump in.

" Don't forget to give me a call Lindsy, and no pressure. My email address is on the back of the paper." Amire quietly and slowly shut the cab door. Both were looking at each other with a slight sadness on their faces now. Amire looking in, and Lindsy out!

" Where to miss? " The broad New York cabby asked.

" Oh, I'm sorry! Springcastle hotel uptown please!" She looked back towards where Amire was stood, but moisture filled her eyes as she saw he was nowhere to be seen.

The emotion of emptiness filled her mind and spirit. Was this the first and last time she would ever see her long lost soul mate? She hoped with all her heart that wouldn't be the case.

The temporary disruption of bodily rhythms by high-speed traveling gave her that jet-lagged feeling as she took items from her suit-cases, then placed them in the hotel rooms closets.

Lindsy directed her mind back to the flight earlier. Another unbelievable occurrence entered her thoughts. The way in which she met Amire.

Sitting quite still on the king size bed, she looked down at the well-made bed linen, then secretly wished that this beautiful man was laying down beside her. Was she being selfish?

Definitely not! Something wonderful had come into her life. Laying on the bed alongside where
she sat her cell phone, passport, and the paper that Amire had left his contact details on.

Her eyes began to feel like lead weights in her head, she needed to sleep and rest her tired and excited body and mind.

After a beautiful contented sleep, she opened her eyes and glanced at the ticking mantal clock. "Thirteen hours! I've slept for thirteen hours." She repeated in her mind.

To wake up fully, she knew that a warm relaxing shower was first on the agenda, then down to the hotel dining room for a well-needed breakfast. The day was well underway as she walked from the hotel to familiarize herself with her new surroundings. Occasionally, she glanced at the boutique's windows, there were so many wonderful things to choose from, she was spoilt for choice, but, this was only the first vacation day, so plenty of time for pampering therapy.

She could see her reflection in darkened window displays. Stopping to see a magnificent evening dress, she knew she had to have it. The label hanging from the garment told her it was a one day sale, it was reduced by forty percent, and at one hundred and fifty dollars, it was a steal. The violet and dark blue dress paraded in the display window, she could visualize herself standing in a dazzling nightclub wearing this.

Entering the boutique, she noticed that it extended at the rear, the large glass sliding doors were another entrance into a well-lit shopping mall. First! She purchased the beautiful dress, then gift wrapping the item, the boutique sales assistant complimented her on her purchase.

" You are very lucky, madam! This particular dress has sold well, you have the last one!"

Thanking the assistant, she picked up the brightly colored boutique bag.

" Welcome to New York Miss!" The lady said and smiled at Lindsy.

The large mall seemed like it went on for hundreds of meters, it had every kind of store
positioned along the entire length.

One particular electrical store had massive savings on fifty-one inch TVs, not really of interest to
Lindsy, but, every screen was running the daily news show.

Staring her right in the face was the tv reporter from the airport the day before.

Amire was giving his short statement, and standing directly beside him was her own image.

She was quite surprised at seeing the news, she was, however, so glad she was smiling at that
point.

"It's you!" Came the words from a young female teenager.

" That was really cool that you helped that guy on the plane. Well done!" She said smiling back
at Lindsy. Blushing a little, she continued to walk along the glittering mall with hundreds of
people also out to snag a bargain or two.

Catching her eye, she noticed a sign for exchanging traveler's cheques, she needed to get some
dollars for her purse and decided this was as good as any to do it.

Joan-Cantor-Amancini! Head bank teller, was the sign on the bank front desk.

" Good morning Madam!" Came the cheerful bubbly voice from behind the desk.

"Welcome to First National Signature Bank. And how may I help you today?"

Her voice was a broad New York accent, almost like the beautiful bubbly female sounds you
 would hear in a cinematic movie.

"And a very good morning to you, Joan! I would like to change some American traveler's
cheques over for cash please!" Lindsy answered in her quiet Swedish accent.
" Of course madam. Ohh! You are the young nurse who helped save that sweet mans life on the
plane yesterday! That was so good of you to help him, and also that Arabic Doctor, What's his
name!? Oh yes! Amire!" She said.
Joan had that wonderful type of personality that you couldn't miss. She had such a way with
conversing with the public, probably why she was at the front desk and was head teller after all.
She continued.
" Wow! Your first day in New York, and famous already!?" She asked and stated in the same
breath.
Lindsy's face began to glow with her blushing hard, then gave a little laugh as she replied to
Joan.
" And all I wanted was to have a quietish vacation."
She replied, then spoke a little more to Joan.
" The emergency on the plane was certainly unexpected, but just recently, I have adapted myself
to weird and wonderful situations arising in my life. Yesterday was no exception to that!"
Joan counted out the two thousand dollars in twenties, then smiled back at Lindsy.
Lindsy had that unusual feeling in her gut again. The feeling that she had met Joan somewhere
before was over-powering.
" Life can certainly throw us some curve balls sometimes, and I feel that you are being guided
towards a wonderful time here on earth." She said still beaming with a beautiful jolly smile.
Then! Her next words surprised Lindsy even more.

" Have you seen your little-feathered friend recently? You know! The red cardinal." Standing
back a bit from her desk, Lindsys eyes opened wider in disbelief at what she was asked.
" Yes, Lindsy, we have met before, but not here in New York. We have met many years ago in a
place you and I would think as Heaven! I know that you are getting to grips with this new way of
life, and I know all of these new things seem pretty crazy, but they do exist! This is just the tip of
the iceberg! Underneath, It's bigger than you could possibly imagine, but oh so beautiful when
we open our eyes and heart wider." Joan's voice and words were so sincere, another beautiful
person put in front of Lindsy's path, and bringing that bright smile back on her face.
" Listen! I'm going to be stopping for my lunch in five minutes! I would love to give you a New-
York welcome and treat you to a meal of your choice! There's a special cozy restaurant along the
mall, and I believe that we might just have a lot in common with our living life!" Before Lindsy
could reply, Joan continued.
" And I'm not taking any other word than yes!" Then added to that sentence.
" So that's settled! I will meet you in about ten minutes at Casio-Italiano. When you exit the
bank, turn right and walk for maybe two hundred meters, tell the Maitre d Geovani the table is
for Joan from the bank. He will give us a private seating area." Surprised, but pleasantly excited,
Lindsy smiled back at her newest friend, then headed for the restaurant.
As she slowly walked the short distance, she was admiring the well-dressed window displays,
and then realized that Joan had said something, " We

knew each other in heaven!!?" "Can this be true?" She asked herself. Like most things that she was experiencing just lately, she once again knew that strange truths were confronting her on a daily basis.

Her world was opening up in ways she could never fully comprehend, but deep down in her heart, she was being gently introduced to a world that was always there but hidden deep until the time was right.

Geovani smiled at Lindsy as she approached the table where he pulled the chair out so she could sit comfortably. " Any friend of Joans, Is certainly mine, too!" He said with a velvet Italian accent.

Sometimes! Movies would feature Italian restaurant scenes, and nearly always have beautiful looking Italian waiters. Geovani was no exception to the rule. He could have been a cat-walk model, with proportionate arm muscles and a very shapely body. He was also around one-hundred and eighty center meters tall, so could also have passed for a bodyguard.

" I saw you on the news bulleting this morning, Lindsy!" He said and had a glowing radiant smile aimed at her.

Geovani returned to the table with a white-clothed fabric around a white wine bottle.

Forcing both his thumbs against the wine cork, he spoke again.

" This is an Italian special white from nineteen fifty-seven, there was only ever five hundred bottles, and this is one of seven I have here in the States!" The cork shot from the opening of the bottle, the popping noise caught the attention of other guests as the cork hit a chandelier above

Lindsy's head.

" Thank you so much, Geovani. I am honored to be one of the lucky ones to taste it!" She replied, and gave him a beautiful Swedish smile back.

" America has been my home for over twenty years, Lindsy, and every now and again, I get to meet wonderful people from all over the world. Today, once again through Joan, a beautiful Swedish lady is in my restaurant. Welcome!" He said pouring the fizzing wine into the long-stemmed glass on her table setting.

Lindsy had to say something cheeky, so replied.

" I bet you say those nice things to all the ladies, Geovani!?" Giving out a quiet laugh.

" Oh! Only to the blond Swedish ones!" He laughed, then winked his right eye towards her.

Even with his posture, he gave out so many charismatic vibrations, it was breathtaking to Lindsy.

" I see you two have met? And, we have the best seats in the restaurant. Oh! A fifty-seven white from Italy? OMG! You are honored!" Joan said laughing and smiling at the same time.

" Be careful, Lindsy! He has his twinkling eyes set on you today!" Joan laughed again and sat down with the helpful Geovani placing the chair under her butt.

" Here is the menu, ladies, we have a wide selection to choose from today, but I recommend the lasagne, its one of my mamma's favorite recipes." Joan chirped up quickly when he mentioned lasagne.

" You must try this Italian dish, Lindsy. If you have never felt a taste of heaven, then you will kiss the hands that made this wonderful cuisine. That's what I would like, Geovani. Lindsy?" Joan glanced over the table to see her nodding her head in agreement as she drank more of the delicious white wine.

" Definitely, Joan. Geovani. Thank you." She replied and placed her nearly empty wine glass
back on the table.

In an instant, he refilled the glass. " Saluti!" Joan said and lifted her empty glass to bring
Both chinking together.

" Did you forget me, sweet Geovani!?" Joan asked.

" Mamma-Mia!! Please forgive me, dear Joan. Mi-Scuzi!"

" I don't blame you, she's very beautiful, and Swedish, too!"

Soft laughter came from their table. Geovani went to prepare their lunch.

" Someone once said. " Stranger things happen at sea." But, there must be many questions racing through your mind, young lady!? All the strangers you have been meeting recently, and weird
and wonderful things that you just can't explain." Joan said.

Lindsy paused for a moment.

" Deep within me, Joan. Everything that has happened, meeting people in strange situations, seeing what most people would say are hallucinations, confuses me, but again somewhere inside
me, there is a library full of information and answers to my questions. Does that make sense,
Joan?" She asked.

Joan had a knowing smile while looking straight at Lindsy's eyes.

" More sense than you could possibly imagine young lady!" She replied.

Topping up her own wine glass, Joan began to sit back in her chair to get more comfortable.

" Lindsy! Today is the first day of the rest of your life. Life as we have known it is just a small sample of what we know. In this beautiful and sometimes cruel world, there are wondrous things happening that evade us, evade us until the time is right to reveal what we need to know. For you! That time is now!"

Looking back over at Joan, Lindsy had a slightly puzzled look, but, again, she knew that honesty was oozing out of Joan's lips.

" There is an old saying, Lindsy! When the pupil is ready, the teacher will come. Especially in your case, that saying means, teachers!"

They both sat back further in their seats as Geovani returned with the magnificent smelling food he placed on the individual place settings.

" Enjoy! And this lunch is on me." He said winking at the two of them.

" Wow! What a sweet guy. One of the good ones I believe!" Joan said. Lindsy agreed with her, then, they started to eat the well-prepared lasagne.

Lindsy was enjoying every moment of her time in the company of Joan. Not being able to put her finger on exactly why she had met this beautiful fifty-five-year-old American beauty, a woman with a smile that would melt ice. She didn't look a day over forty, her dark shoulder length hair rested on the base of her neck. Joan was one of these wonderful human beings that if put in a crowd of a hundred people, she would stand out like a bright red rose among the lighter colored carnations.

" First dear Lindsy. I don't do this very often, in fact, probably spaces of three or five years can elapse between what I call lessons. Sometimes, people come into my life, just like the ways

things are happening to you, and, I spiritually grow closer to the hidden energy that surrounds
our entire being. When the heart is being honest with the present day, amazing things present
themselves in stunning and mysterious ways." Every second, every word that uttered from Joan's
mouth, angelic type vibrations would penetrate Lindsy's body, her thoughts, and not least, her
heart.
Single words were sounding like melodies in the open mountain ranges, they held a certain
harmonious effect. Native American flute music could have been attached to the words, and
undertones of a beautiful wolf cry.
Not for one moment did Lindsy think Joan was some kind of hypnotist, but every word was
hypnotic. Joan spoke deep from her heart. Lindsy could also sense a slight loss in Joan's aura,
 like someone wonderful was missing from her soul. No sooner than Lindsy had those thoughts,
Joan answered.
" Let me tell you a little about me, Lindsy. There was a wonderful man in my life who I was
married to. He was my daily sunshine, my love food, and more than anything, my soulmate!"
Joan's eyes could be seen to emit tears from each corner of the eye sockets. Choking back her
moist droplets, she reached for her napkin, then wiped away the dripping water. Composing
herself more, she continued to tell Lindsy a little of the love story from her life.
" I'm sorry! Lindsy. After all these years, you would think I could hold a conversation about my
dear husband without tearing up!" She said.
" We all remember what happened that dreadful day in September two thousand and one. Better

known as 9/11. I'm just one of those people in the world who cried for all those souls who lost
their lives not far from here. Television coverage could only show you a fraction of what was
 happening, people running for cover and fleeing as best they could from that horrific terrorist
attack. All the emergency services racing towards the danger, and some heroes who helped
people laying in the streets, some were hit by debris, their faces were telling a horror story, but
the worst as we know was still to come."
Lindsy had changed her facial expression to shock as she continued to listen to one persons
horrible account of that day's events.
" Panic set in very quickly when I realized my husband worked very close to the World Trade
Center! After both towers had fallen, a cold icy feeling engulfed my entire body, but, somehow
knew he was alive. I heard a very soothing voice in my mind, it was saying that my husband was
safe, and he would call as soon as he was able.! Was the voice, God? I believe it was! God as I
understand him. A powerful divine energy that struck my heart with a bolt of love-light! My
anxiety subsided very quickly, then a peace surrounded me that is nearly impossible to describe.
I was connected to a force, a force so full of love that it vibrated strongly in my mind and body."
Joan described sad scenes from that day.
" My husband managed to call fifty minutes later. Because of the voice, I let go, I knew that God
would help get him back to me.
I believe that thousands of dear souls found their way to heaven that day! But, that day, my
husband was spared!
A few months later, he was diagnosed with an illness

caused by the inhalation of toxic dust that
had mixed with the atmosphere that day. I found out
he had gone into areas where people were
running from, and helped as many needy people as
possible. Not long after the diagnosis, he lost
his battle for life. When he passed, he left a hole
deep inside me, a hole the size of the Grand
Canyon."
Lindsy held her hands up to her face, rubbing her
teary eyes. She felt every ounce of pain in
Joan's words.
" Here comes the best news from that situation
though! Day by day, weeks turned into months,
then years. I had visions, yes! Visions! Visions of my
husband standing in front of me.
Only, he was standing there as real as you and I are
here now.
He had a golden glow surrounding him, he stood
there with one of the most wonderful smiles
you could imagine. Seeing him was so beautiful, but
when he spoke to me, it was like all the love
he had ever felt for me was projected to my warm
beating heart."
As Joan continued to tell Lindsy about this wonderful
man who was in her life, she had a glow
about her, her aura extended more around her body.
Her eyes sparkled as she spoke of her soul
mate.
" Antonio was an angel in human form! He still is!
Every now and again, he visits me, mainly
when I'm sitting on the bed. He gently floats around
the bottom of the bed, he smiles that
Antonio smile, then gently fades away.
For a few moments each time he appears, he
reminds me of the deep love I also have for him.
There was one occasion just recently, a golden

transparent eagle appeared at the base of my bed,
but, I knew that it was Antonio in his animal totem!
The glistening eagle eyes were his!
He sent subliminal messages to me just the other
day. The message was this. The shining blond
Swedish girl is your new pupil. Wrap her up in all that
love you have in your heart, then place
her gently on the new path in front of her. Tell her
the red cardinal will never betray her. When
the warm-blooded bird speaks, believe what she
hears, as the path to her future will reveal itself
quickly!"
Lindsy's eyes had opened a little wider as Joan
continued to tell her this amazing story.
" Love will always find a heart to attach to, Lindsy!
Love can be an easy word that most people
will never know the true meaning of, but, to feel love,
is to know pure heaven! Now is the time
you will feel all that love, you are meant to receive."
Lindsy focused all her gaze on Joan. Once again,
Lindsy was unbelievably intrigued at what the
wonderful woman was saying.
" I'm going to stretch my neck out a little more now,
and I'm going to say that this wonderful
doctor you have met truly is your soulmate! He's a
gift sent from heaven, just like you are to him.
I know you feel that within your heart already Lindsy!
There is a glowing spark in you so bright,
he was attracted to you like a moth to a flame!
Whatever you do, don't give up the chance of true
love with this man. You both are joined at the heart,
and also your untainted souls." Joan said,
then reached once again for the delicious wine.
Lindsy had so many questions she wanted to ask her,
but had no idea where to begin. As if by
magic telepathy, Joan answered her thoughts.

" Today! Has just been the start of all the beautiful things yet to come. Today is the day that you know you're no longer alone. You never have been, but sometimes you felt that was the way it was. I know you have hundreds of questions for me, Lindsy, and I want to answer them all, for that, I would like to invite you to my home over on Staten Island. Of course, I will prepare a special meatloaf for you. Can't have you going back to Sweden without tasting my meatloaf." She laughed, then continued. " And, no! You don't get to say, No!!" Both of them gave out a hearty laugh.

Time was seeming to pass quickly as Joan looked at her watch.

" I need to get back to work in a moment, but here is my cell number and address. I finish work

tomorrow at five, so maybe you can meet me at the bank? I will prepare the food tonight so only a short while will be needed to cook when we get home."

Joan reached out to pull Lindsy closer to her, she gave the biggest tight hug possible. Pulses of energy invisibly ran between both of their bodies, Lindsy felt safe next to this beautiful woman.

Waking up the second day after a fantastic peaceful sleep, Lindsy smiled to herself as she remembered the great previous day. Her memory jumped into a calm action, as she computed the conversations the new friends had.

Lindsy raised from her chair once again as she was in need of a caffeine fix. Writing in her secret diary was enjoyable, but every now and again she needed that little extra boost to help her

continue with her exciting story.
Holding the warm to touch mug of hot chocolate, and also topped with whipped cream, she stood
in the twilight early evening. The golden yellows, pinks, reds, and not forgetting the wonderful
powder blue sky. The sun was now beginning to lower beyond the horizon, this sunset was what
she needed to see, to remind her that love was coming in many ways, not just in human forms.
As she passed her computer desk on the other side of the living room, she smiled again to herself
as she knew that in a few hours, she would gladly use this modern piece of equipment to talk to
Joan. The time difference was inconvenient at times, but, speaking and seeing Joan in real time
thousands of miles apart was incredible. Lindsy after all these weeks returning to Sweden had
started to use her laptop, more now than in the couple of years she had owned it. The four
thousand mile gap became nonexistent.
Placing the remains of her chocolate mug next to her diary, Lindsy lifted her trusty pen, pushing
the ballpoint against the paper, she continued with that episode in her life.

Joan and Lindsy jumped down the short distance from the bus as they reached a beautiful part of
Staten Island.
Snug Harbor cultural park was the name on the sign next to where they alighted the bus.
" This is so different to uptown New York Lindsy, it's like another world here! The history
museum has many interesting things to see, so I thought for an hour or so before dinner, we
could take in some of the good things Staten Island has to offer, and you can then say to your

family and friends " You saw some of the other sides
of New York!" I come here when I can, to
gather that bit of inner peace I feel when I'm here.
It's a perfect end to a work day."
Lindsy felt a warm glow surround her as she looked
at the park, then surveyed the white marbled
old building, with new additions.
" When I come here, Lindsy! I can imagine Abraham
Lincoln walking among the tall trees and
wonderful flower beds. I feel the difference between
what was then in his time, to now! I wonder
what he might say about America now? Would he be
proud? Or would he be saddened by the
very fast growing land we call America?" Joan
thought for a moment, then answered herself.
" I think he might be pleased, but maybe a little sad
at the way some of the world has tried to
destroy our free way of life. But! As we live day by
day, we have to continue and cultivate a love
that will help heal our lands. That's what we should
put first before anything. A love that reaches
every heart by doing kindness to those in unfortunate
situations, people who can't enjoy their
lives as well as we do. I'm sorry! I chatter too much
at times!" She said, then directed Lindsy
towards the very large museum door.
About forty minutes passed walking around the old
museum. It was then that Joan glanced at
her watch.
" Dinner should be cooking as we speak. Its great to
have modern equipment turn on by itself!
Oh! And one more thing. I have someone else
coming to dinner, this guy is going to surprise
you. I won't tell you anything about who he is, it will
be a nice surprise when we get to my
home." There it was again! That beautiful knowing

trademark of a smile she had.

" Now I'm really intrigued!" Lindsy laughed with her reply.

After a brisk walk from the park, both the women strolled into a very smart housing area. Each house was adequately spaced, so not to give that cramped feeling.

As they approached a two-level white and grey house, Lindsy knew this was belonging to Joan. Outside the front of the building, a triple row of flowers lit up the base of the white wall.

Standing proudly against the brickwork was a row of pure white rose bushes. The center row was bright crimson and the third row at the front towards them was another pure white line of roses.

The few steps in front of them extended upwards to a decking type porch. There were two separately placed varnished rocking chairs slightly facing each other. The gentle breath of a cool wind rocked them.

A wonderful aroma drifted through the nooks and crevices of the wooden front door.

" Wow! That smells delicious, Joan!" Lindsy said looking at her hosts face.

" That dish was one of my husband's favorites when I cooked it for him, we used to sit here on the rockers, take in all of the evenings bright sunsetting colors, and go over our day. We sometimes would play footsie while we rocked back and then forward, our feet would bounce gently as they touched, then sometimes, we would take turns to catch each others foot with both of the ones who were doing the catching." She said. Her face was smiling, there was no sadness written upon it. A wonderful memory skipped through

her mind as she looked at the moving
antique rockers.
The sound of a honking car horn interupted their
chain of thought as they both turned to see an
old customized Ford Mustang turning into the
driveway.
" And this! Young Lindsy is John-Yellow-Wolf-Mobern!
As you can see by his appearance, he
is of Native American origin. You are going to be so
overwhelmed by this fascinating man."
Lindsy gently took hold of the mans hand, she held it
tightly to shake it, then, the incredible
energies flowed through her entire being.
" I wasn't surprised when Joan telephoned me
yesterday, Lindsy. I have been expecting you!"
He moved closer to Lindsy, and without warning,
gave her one of the friendliest hugs anyone
could receive. John stepped back a little, then
continued.
" I had a spiritual encounter some weeks back now,
Lindsy. I was meditating in my Teepee.
After a few moments connecting to the universe, I
was guided to a fluffy cloudy sky was
floating around me was some of the natures finest
feathered creatures. One, in particular, was
that of a Red Cardinal. Imagine my surprise when I
started to communicate telepathically with
this little bird. He began to go into great detail about
a blond Swedish girl who would soon travel
to my homeland! She would cross the vast ocean to
learn of the distant path she had traveled, and
I was to enlighten her on some of the most amazing
secrets in our world!" John couldn't resist
hugging her again, then continued.
" That food smells divine Joan!" He said ushering the
two girls through the now opened door.

" After dinner, we can talk about all the wonderful things that have happened, and some of the great things still to happen! And one very special event that will change your life forever!"
Topping up Lindsy's wine glass, then her own, Joan sat back down and spoke to John.
" I know you only drink water at the dinner table, John! But, you know you can have a stiff glass of Scotch whiskey later! One of your special highland malts! The one you call Fire Water!" Each one of them laughed, then John replied.
" Yes! It's certainly firewater. I know if I drink any of those, I will be frequenting the spare bedroom tonight." Again he laughed out loud as they all raised their individual glasses and toasted each other.
Time could have stood still after the wonderfully cooked meatloaf. Time was allowing the three of them to talk about the individual paths they had traveled. The universe was vast, it was paving the way for them to have as much conversation as possible. If there had been an observer watching the three of them, he would describe the following scenes.
" The downstairs living area was warm and inviting. At either side of the unlit fireplace, stood glass, brass and flame retardant strong paper wrapped around four feet high imitation angel wings. Each one pointing away from the center of the fire. With white glowing mini bulbs lighting the structures, they gave the impression of an angel with a bright aura lighting up the entire room.
Each one of the three also had silvery gold auras jutting out to about three feet. Each aura in the shape of an egg! Each one looking like it had broken

loose from the flame of a crackling fire.
The atmosphere was electric as thousands of charged
particles danced around the room.
There was a feeling of pure un-tainted love emitting
from each human soul! These three were
the type of thing you would be drawn to! Positivity
breeds positivity, and love in its purest form
does the exact same. If I was to enter this beautiful
home, I know that the love that was
surrounding them would be infectious!"
John sat back on the comfortable couch, his athletic
looking body sank into the cushioned fabric
as he nursed his sparkling crystal glass of whiskey.
" Now! Ladies!" He said still smiling.
" I have known of amazing happenings in my
lifetime. I believe something so wonderful is going
to happen very soon, I don't have an exact time
frame of when, but, it is going to take place this
year. I have been told by my guardian angel a new
dawn is breaking in the world. The world as
we know it will be charged with an energy so
powerful, people all over the world will gasp as to
the power this will emit!
Sometimes! This great world of ours needs a gentle
nudge in the right direction. In this next
phase of the world, it's going to be more of a giant
push!" Still smiling, John continued.
" Do you know who you are! Lindsy?" John asked
looking straight at her shining eyes.
" Or should I say. Do you know what you are?"
Silence fell in the room, but if working brain
cells had sounded, it was deafening!
After just a few seconds thinking, Lindsy answered
his questions.
" John! I know something very strange has entered
my life in a very short time frame. I have

been more in tune with unseen energies, colors, beautiful realistic dreams, and feelings of what
 I can only describe as pure love! I also believe I have been given some special healing gifts,
gifts which have proven to work beyond modern technology. I think that I'm treading on the
correct path, it just feels right!"
Joan had been sitting listening quietly as John and Lindsy spoke back and forth to each other.
Her face glowed brightly with a knowing smile.
John once again continued while sipping slowly the malt Scotch whiskey.
He focused his eyes on the golden liquid sitting in his glass.
" When I see this liquid before me, I see a golden glow reflected by the light of the room. I know
that when I take a little into my mouth, a great taste can be felt to start with. When it swirls
around inside, my tongue detects the flavor. When my brain works out that its good for me in
small quantities, I swallow gently to let the wonderful specially brewed Scotch to enter the pit of
my stomach. After only a couple of seconds, my internal body starts to analyze what has just
taken place. Like a brand new fire being lit, the warm glow gets stronger and then stronger
as each sip of the liquid fuels that ever glowing light inside me. Does that make sense, Lindsy?"
He asked.
Lindsy returned the smile. She knew exactly what John was saying. He was describing her new
spiritual awakening. He lifted the glass to his lips once again, rested it on his lap, and continued.
" I think you are beginning to grasp a new way of life for yourself, young lady. If you only take
little sips of the liquid, which in your case is spiritual

energy, it will ignite a flame so bright,
people will need sunglasses to shield their eyes from
your brightness." Yet again all three gently
 laughed.
" Here on Staten Island. There are special spiritual
Ley-Lines. Believed to be special spiritual
points where a straight line runs between hotspots.
These hotspots are charged allegedly with
unlimited energy of light, a light that can be felt, as
well as a divine power. This power is only
filled with the purest love. Therefore! Only the purest
of spirits can project themselves to one of
the special points. Joan knows that this very house is
built on one of the special Ley-Lines. At
the very center of this house, a vortex of pure light,
invisible to us with our naked eyes, but when
we open our hearts, we can see it as clear as day."
John placed his glass on the small coffee
table in front of him, then closed his eyes, raised his
arms like a lot of Native Americans do just
before praying to the great spirit. God! As each
individual understood God to mean.
" Great God! Please allow the circle of divine light to
shine in this room. Protect us with your
light and wisdom. Allow us to see and feel the love
that you are giving to us. Let no harm come
to anyone here present."
There was a silence, a silence with charged energy
surrounding them. All three after John uttered
those words could feel some kind of shift in the
particles of air.
All three pairs of eyes now were focusing on a room
that began to brighten. Every corner of the
living room was no longer in a shadow. Then, it
happened.
Materializing in front of them was an eight foot in

diameter spiraling circle of sparkling silvery
white light.
Joan smiled a knowing smile, this wasn't the first time
she had experienced this type of spinning
vortex of light. Lindsy smiled but had her mouth
slightly open in amazement as the white light
spun.
The light began to emit a faint humming, like a
magical hidden vibrational tone. Where all three
sat, no one wanted to move. Their eyes fixed on the
inside of the circle of light.
Pulsating waves of moving bright colors cascaded
around the outer circle, then falling to the
center of the inner space.
Lindsy couldn't bear to take her eyes off the light, she
was afraid if she did, she would miss
something spectacular. She would have been right.
For the next few moments, wave after wave
of color bounced and dove towards the inside ring of
light.
Whispering transparent streaks of color and white
light flowed from the outer circle. Every pair
of eyes were fixed on the dancing lights.
When they reached their bodies, each flowing color
wrapped and swirled around them like a
security blanket.
Pulsating and penetrating their entire being,
emotional happiness, feelings of serenity, and
the peace that was better felt than explained.
John knew what was to follow, he smiled over at the
two women. He spoke his next words
quietly.
" And now, the best is yet to come. Keep your eyes
on the center of the circle, you are both in for
the treat of your life!" Still with a smile beaming
around his face.

Recently, Lindsy had begun to open her eyes as to
strange occurrences, and this one was no
different.
Again, seconds seemed to last minutes, almost like
time was slowing down. With a new look at
 her recent perception of life, Lindsy was beginning to
open her mind to anything was possible
mode.
Suddenly! A purge of cobalt blue energized light filled
the inside of the circling light.
Each of their eyes was squinting now, straining to
see through the bright blue and white light.
A hint of a shadow could be seen forming right in the
middle of the circling vortex.
With every second, the shadow began to take the
shape of a human form.
With more seconds ticking by, the shape was
beginning to resemble a woman. This woman was
standing bare feet in the circle. Her hair was shoulder
length and silvery blond.
As she manifested more, each one of them could see
she was beginning to smile.
An even brighter light shon from the back of her
neck. Almost like a heavenly aura
Surrounding her near perfect body.
When she was fully formed in front of them, they
saw that she was naked from head to foot.
Lindsy smiled as she gazed at one of the most
beautiful women she had ever seen.
Still saying to herself at times. " Is this really
happening? "

Back in her apartment, Lindsy put the pen down on
top of her diary, she needed to stretch her
legs and body before continuing. Reaching over to a
half-filled bottle of red wine she poured the

flowing liquid slowly into her crystal stemmed glass.
There was such a wonderful feeling as she thought of
that special moment when this attractive
 woman became visible to her astonished eyes.
Staring over at the living room clock, she walked over
to the desktop computer, It was time to
talk to her wonderful new friend, Joan!
" Hey!! Glad to see you, young lady, spot on time as
usual. " Joan said as her real-time webcam
Projected her smiling face on to Lindsy's computer
screen. Joan continued.
" So what are you doing today? " She asked.
Laughing out loud, Lindsy replied.
" Oh! I'm just writing in my secret diary, I am at the
part where you, John and I are just seeing
the naked woman." Joan laughed at the same time as
Lindsy.
" That was a fantastic night, and was breathtaking
when she appeared," Joan answered.
For a second or two, Lindsy paused, then said.
" I am still overwhelmed at everything I experienced
back in the states. Every day I think of
pinching myself, just to make sure I'm not in a
dream." Again Joan laughed.
" I know! Lindsy. And soon you will be on your travels
again."
" Yep! But I haven't mentioned any of that yet!" It
was Lindsy's turn to laugh, that all-knowing
laugh.
Every time they managed to speak to each other,
Lindsy could always see that glowing aura
Which surrounded Joans moving real-time image.
Like a magnet pulling on her eyes, Lindsy loved every
second of her time catching up with
Joan. This was now a regular occurrence, sometimes
three times a week.

" How is the travel arrangements going for your journey to Apangistan? " Joan asked chuckling into the microphone.

" Done! I fly from Stockholm in six days, I am so excited to get to see a brand new country I have never been to."

" Yayyy!" Joan replied waving her hands from side to side in front of the webcam.

" Is that liquid courage you are drinking? " Joan asked. She continued.

" Seeing you with that glass of wine is making me thirsty." She laughed.

" Its great to be writing my memoirs and relaxing for a while with this red wine, but not as good as the wine we had back in New York! Huh?" They both laughed simultaneously.

Each time they managed to get chatting, their invisible bond grew stronger and stronger. Sometimes, they both felt a powerful connection, a connection that gave them the impression they were two peas from the same pod, so to speak.

" I wish that I was going with you, Lindsy. But! I have the feeling the universe has something big lined up for me, and sooner rather than later. I guess I will find out soon enough." She said, with a melting smile.

Lindsy waisted no time in replying to her dear older friend.

" Oh my dear Joan. I would have loved to have you with me, and who knows? One day, you will be next to me looking at the wonderful visions in front of us!"

Time was catching up slowly, and Joan had to return to her place of work at the bank.

" So! My sweet Lindsy. Need to dash away again, but will talk to you just before you leave in a few days. " Both at the same time, they waved and blew kisses.

The computer screen returned to its standby mode, then, flickered to the off position.

Lindsy felt great as she stared at the black screen for a moment. Her smile was still reflecting back at her.

" Ok! " She said to herself. " I'm refreshed and ready to continue writing."

She picked up the last drops of wine in her glass, swallowed the liquid slowly, then walked the short distance to her diary, sat down and once again lifted her trusty pen.

" We welcome you into this wonderful light and living room. We thank you for giving us the time to help us in our journeys. " John spoke those words with such beautiful bass tones, and Lindsy could have sworn that the words echoed with a strong vibration making her heart center jump slightly.

At that moment, words came from the shining naked lady as the light spun around her.

Her hair seemed to flow a little blowing with a slight breeze inside the circle.

" I am Jasmin! I extend the love of the divine creator. He sent me to be your guide! "

Her voice could only be described as angelic! Her womanly high voice echoed around the entire room. A feeling of serenity engulfed the three friends. Lindsy glanced over at Joan, she saw that she had tears trickling down her cheeks. These tears were tears of joy, not sadness. This was so incredible to witness such happenings.

As all three of them listened to the glowing entity standing before them.

" What you see around me is a divine light that

makes it possible for me to be here with you at
this very moment. Many of us have asked to be with
many of you to help the shift in the worlds
consciousness. The God of your understanding or not
understanding has chosen each one of you
on the earth plane to put into motion the change for
the greater good of mankind.
Some of you have discovered some of the beautiful
gifts which have been given to you. It is time
in the earth's cycle of growth to shift to a higher form
of conscious thinking." Every word she
spoke was so sincere, every word rang true to each
of them. They didn't need any proof of what
she was saying, they just knew that her honesty
didn't need to be questioned.
I guess It might have been odd looking to anyone
that might have been looking in on the
circling bright light, and a naked woman standing
with flowing hair in an unseen breeze.
But! Only the three of them could see her.
Jasmin continued.
" A great wind will grow into a chaotic storm in a
faraway land, and each one of you will help in
ways you might think impossible. You will know what
to do when that time comes. The outcome
will prove to you that there are more things to
connect to than you can possibly imagine. You
will never be alone in the darkest hours. Look for the
light, and you will find that light." Jasmin
once again smiled at each one of them. She looked
back at Lindsy and beckoned to her to join
her in the circle.
A little apprehensive at first, then took courage to
raise herself from her seat, she walked slowly
towards the glowing bright spinning light.
A cool chill enveloped Lindsy as she passed through

the outside circle of light. A few steps
further in and she walked through every color flowing
through and over her body, mind, and
soul.
As she breathed in the colored lights, she slowly
started to feel tingling sensations and like every
cell in her body was dancing to the free floating
colors.
Jasmin reached out to hold Lindsys hand. It felt so
strange as a warm-blooded ghostly type figure
guided her a few steps.
Suddenly! Lindsy noticed that the room had
dissapeared from the outer circle. In its place,
hundreds of thousands of stars in the distance. Still
feeling the ground beneath her feet, but, as
she looked down, there was no ground, no floor
boards. In three-hundred and sixty degrees, she
was in the vast darkness of space.
Headed towards them was a large tunnel of light. It
spanned at least one-hundred meters in
Diameter. The light surrounding the tunnel was like a
cascading firework with emitting sparks.
It was like watching a warp speed light heading
straight for them. No way would it miss them.
Lindsy had another calmness come over her, she
looked over at Jasmin and her returned look
had a knowing and awsome smile, but then again,
she knew what was coming next…………

                                             END OF
PART 1
                        WORDS FROM AN ANGEL BY PETER
JAMES LJUNG

                              PART 2 TO BE RELEASED
FALL/WINTER 2019

Lightning Source UK Ltd.
Milton Keynes UK
UKRC031958070223
416655UK00014B/308/J